A Caroling Christmas

Julie Warnick

Covenant Communications, Inc.

ALSO BY JULIE WARNICK:

Light of Bethlehem

One Silent Night

Cover illustration © Jess Hager. By arrangement with Mill Pond Licensing, Venice, FL 34285.
For information on art prints by Jess Hager, please call Mill Pond Press at 800-535-0331.

Cover design copyrighted 2004 by Covenant Communications, Inc.

Published by Covenant Communications, Inc.
American Fork, Utah

Copyright © 2004 by Julie A. Warnick

All rights reserved. No part of this book may be reproduced in any format or in any medium without the written permission of the publisher, Covenant Communications, Inc., P.O. Box 416, American Fork, UT 84003. The views expressed herein are the responsibility of the author and do not necessarily represent the position of Covenant Communications, Inc.

This is a work of fiction. The characters, names, incidents, places, and dialogue are products of the author's imagination, and are not to be construed as real.

Printed in Canada
First Printing: October 2004

10 09 08 07 06 05   10 9 8 7 6 5 4 3 2

ISBN 1-59156-674-6

DEDICATION

To my grandparents, Howard Nielson and the late Julia Nielson. They started the caroling tradition in our family over forty years ago and have left a legacy of kindness and service for all of their posterity. I am grateful for their fine examples.

ACKNOWLEDGMENTS

I would like to thank my husband Quin. I appreciate the many times you have taken our daughters on special outings so that I could have time to write. Also, thank you for giving me the idea to write this story and helping me throughout the process. Your support and love mean everything to me.

Thanks to my daughters, Emily and Hannah, for being patient while Mommy types on the computer from time to time. Your sweet smiles and hugs bring me more happiness than you'll ever know.

To my parents, Steve and Noreen Astin, thank you again for taking the time out of your busy schedules to read and proof the various drafts of this story. Your corrections and suggestions have been invaluable to me. Thank you for believing in me.

Finally, I would like to acknowledge Shauna Humphreys and Angela Colvin of Covenant Communications. I have learned so much from both of you.

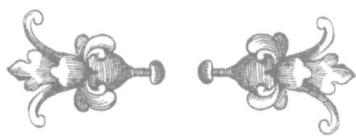

I'm not going caroling," Carl stated, hoping to put an end to the argument that had consumed the morning.

"It's a Christmas tradition," Annie said quietly, staring intently at the wood grain in the kitchen table. "We do it every year."

"Well then, by all means, you should go." Carl shoveled a bite of soggy cornflakes into his mouth and focused his attention back on the morning paper.

"I plan to, but . . . " Annie paused, then took a deep breath. "It would mean a lot to me if you would come too." She eyed her husband warily, but he didn't look up to meet her gaze. "And everyone will ask where you are. I don't want to make excuses anymore."

"Excuses?" Carl asked sarcastically, finally looking up from the sports section. "You can tell them *I* have work to do. The stacks of paperwork on my desk are not going to vanish into thin air. And no little Christmas elf is going to magically finish my reports over the weekend. If I don't stay late tonight, I'll be behind all next week." He instinctively left out the part about wanting to watch his favorite team play later that evening.

"You managed to come home early last Friday," Annie said evenly, though her dark eyes were smoldering. "When What's-his-name at the office came up with extra tickets to the game."

"Last Friday!" He slammed the paper on the table and stood abruptly. Annie also rose from her seat, her fiery glare threatening to pierce a hole right through him. "*What's-his-name at the office*, whose name is Brian, wasn't trying to convince me to *waste* an entire evening making a fool of myself."

"So, that's how you feel." Annie fought to control her voice. "Going to a ball game is worth your time . . . and being with my family isn't. At least you finally admitted it."

"No, I didn't say that," he began, grateful he'd kept quiet about the upcoming game. "You always put words in my mouth. But, since we're talking about my *feelings*, I'll tell you—not that it will matter. I don't *feel* like going to a bunch of old people's houses, especially when I don't even know them." He took his seat. Annie remained standing, her face suddenly like stone. "Besides, I'm just not like you and your family. All that singing and stuff makes me feel like an idiot. We're just different."

"You know, I've been thinking about that a lot," Annie said after a long pause. "We are different—maybe a little too different." Her eyes, suddenly filled with sadness, met his for a brief moment. Then she turned and walked out of the kitchen.

"What is that supposed to mean?" Carl called after her retreating back, but there was no response.

* * *

Hanging back from the rest of the group, Carl wished he could disappear into the biting December air. As the evening wore on, his mood, already sour from the morning argument, was going from bad to worse. Trudging through the snow with Annie's relatives, many of whom he barely knew, wasn't making him feel any better. And the throbbing in his head from the events of the afternoon was getting harder to ignore. Carl had left work an hour early, maneuvered his way on icy roads, and fought bumper-to-bumper traffic. *And for what?* he wondered angrily. He had barely made it home before Annie left, and the reception she had given him was less than warm. The surprised look on her face had been fleeting, only to be replaced by a frosty expression colder than the weather outside. She hadn't spoken more than two words to him on the way to her grandparents' house.

"Let's just get through this as smoothly as possible," Annie had said as they'd arrived. "You know, keep up appearances. I'm not up to answering any questions tonight." Carl had nodded silently while she plastered on her best smile and took him by the arm to join her family.

"Here come the two lovebirds!" Annie's younger brother had called out, causing both of them to cringe inwardly.

Now Carl wondered why he was there at all. His feelings about caroling hadn't changed, but Annie's final words that morning had bothered him enough to seek advice from Brian at work that day.

"Happy wife, happy life!" Brian had said, confiding his secret for marital bliss with Carl. "If you go, she'll be happy—things will be good as new. And who knows? Just maybe a little more Christmas spirit will do you some good!" He had slugged Carl playfully in the shoulder. "You can handle it big guy—it's just one night."

Well, Brian was wrong on all three counts, Carl thought miserably. To begin with, Annie was still mad. The whole mess hadn't blown over like he'd hoped, and things between them were far from good as new. Secondly, he wasn't in need of any more Christmas spirit. Carl liked Christmas well enough and enjoyed the festivities that went along with it. He didn't mind "decking the halls" and even doing things for other people. He just wasn't into *this* kind of holiday tradition. And last, but definitely not least, he wasn't sure if he really could handle one night of caroling. He hadn't felt so miserably awkward in a very long time.

Doesn't anyone else think this is ridiculous? Carl thought, looking at the jovial bunch ahead of him. The adults bantered back and forth as they walked, while numerous children giggled and dodged each other's snowballs over snow-covered lawns and sidewalks. He winced as someone ahead of him began boisterously singing "We Wish You a Merry Christmas." *Guess not,* he concluded dismally.

"We're so happy you could join us!" Carl's mother-in-law said, squeezing his arm affectionately.

Carl forced a grin and nodded. He certainly wasn't happy about it, especially when the game was starting in less than an hour. Last week's game had been a nail-biter to say the least. The score was tied when the clock ran out; but, in the end, his team had squeaked by—winning in overtime. Tonight they were again up against stiff competition, which promised to be very exciting. It was killing him to miss it.

The game in front of me, maybe some chips and salsa, he thought wistfully. *That would sure beat being out in this miserable stuff!* He looked down in disgust at his brand-new shoes, already wet and soggy from tromping through the snowy neighborhood. The icy moisture was beginning to seep through his socks and bite at his skin. Before long most of the feeling in his toes would be gone, only to be replaced by the dull ache of his numbed lower extremities. Grunting softly, he shoved his hands deeper into the pockets of his coat. It was going to be a long night.

Annie pulled him to a stop in front of a large brick home adorned with colorful, blinking lights and a jolly Santa in the middle of the front lawn. A tall, decorated tree glittered grandly through the front window. Music could be heard from within.

What are we doing here? Carl thought indignantly, his irritation rising to a whole new level. Annie had said they would be visiting the lonely and cheering the afflicted. There was no evidence of loneliness or need at this home. Now he was sure the whole event was a waste of time.

Yet the group, in Carl's opinion, seemed oblivious to the obvious. After a brief conference, a child was sent with a plate of sloppily wrapped goodies to ring the doorbell. Wishing he could duck underneath the boughs of the large evergreen looming beside him, Carl stared at the door. It opened promptly.

"Ah, it's the Wilsons!" a middle-aged man called over his shoulder cheerfully, then turned back to face his visitors. "How have you been?"

"Fine, just fine, Brother Marshall!" Annie's grandpa, the patriarch of the Wilson family, replied heartily. "We're here to wish you a Merry Christmas and sing a carol or two."

Just then a woman, whom Carl assumed was Sister Marshall, appeared at the door.

"Oh, come inside quickly!" she exclaimed without hesitation. "It's positively freezing out there!" She began pulling those closest to her into the house, as if she were rescuing them from certain death.

"What are we doing?" Carl whispered, looking at Annie in surprise. *We aren't really going to squeeze everyone into the house, are we?* he thought, panic seizing him. *Is that necessary? Don't carolers traditionally sing at the doorstep?*

"Everyone invites us in," Annie said flatly, ignoring Carl's shock. Then, without another word, she propelled him toward the door.

Everyone invites us in? This can't be happening! Carl brooded silently, completely crestfallen as the realization sunk in. This ordeal was going to take even longer than he anticipated—all hope of watching any of the game faded into the miserably cold evening.

Once inside, Carl tried to make his way to the back of the room where he wouldn't be noticed, but it was impossible. The Wilsons were packed in so tightly around him that he could barely breathe, let alone sing even if he had wanted to—which he didn't. The close quarters didn't dampen the spirit of the Wilson family, however. On cue, they burst simultaneously into song with their rendition of "Joy to the World." There was nothing Carl could do but try to keep up and hope that no one could hear him.

The Marshalls cheered and clapped when the carol was over.

"You sound just like a choir of angels!" Sister Marshall exclaimed.

"Oh, you're too kind," Grandpa Wilson replied humbly. "Before we leave, we would like to sing one more—especially for your mother." He continued, but more slowly and articulately. "Sister Schmidt, we would like to sing 'Silent Night' for you." It was then that Carl noticed the silver-haired woman rocking quietly in the corner of the room. She was smiling and nodding, but did not speak. Sister Marshall whispered something to her mother that Carl couldn't hear. Her mother's smile widened, and an expectant look filled her eyes.

"Please join us," Grandpa suggested to the Marshalls.

At the end of the fourth verse, the group fell silent, except for the tenor voices of Taylor and Adam, two of the Wilson sons.

"Stille nacht, heilige nacht . . ." The sound of "Silent Night" sung in German filled the house. With the help of a sturdy wooden cane, Sister Schmidt slowly stood up from the corner rocking chair. Her face glowed as she joined in, singing the hallowed song in her native tongue. Though her body was aged and bent, her voice was clear and strong—filled with such reverence that even the children were spellbound.

The last note hovered, then faded away, leaving the room in silence. Sister Schmidt carefully made her way to Taylor and Adam, then hugged them tightly.

"Danke," she said, thanking the group in her language. Her voice was slow and deliberate. Then, turning back to the Wilson sons, she began conversing easily with them in German. Sister Schmidt's expressions were lively and animated as they talked back and forth.

Now the reason for coming to the Marshall home was clear. Sister Schmidt could not speak English. Taylor and Adam had served missions in her homeland and were able to bring Christmas cheer in a language she could understand.

"Mom, what *are* they talking about?" a small, freckle-faced boy asked loudly, his nose scrunched up in confusion. This brought a smile to everyone, even Carl. He tousled the boy's blond hair, feeling just a bit sorry that he couldn't understand what was being said either.

"Oh, you dear people," Sister Marshall said at the conclusion of the visit. "This means so much to Mother—thank you."

Farewells were said, then out into the cold the group went.

"Was that *so* horrible?" Annie asked Carl with just a hint of sarcasm.

"It wasn't that bad," he replied, not wanting to make a scene, but at the same time feeling annoyed all over again. *At least it wouldn't be so bad if we only had to go to one house,* he grumbled silently. *But to spend an entire evening . . . doing nothing but singing?*

It still sounded bad to him. Carl hadn't been raised like Annie. He hadn't spent evenings singing around the piano, and he hadn't taken choir classes in high school or college. Singing in harmony or reading music was as foreign to him as the German he'd just heard. He couldn't even remember the last time he had sung in the shower. The fact was that not everyone liked to sing. Why couldn't Annie understand that? Why was she always trying to change him?

Sure, it was nice to visit Sister Schmidt, Carl concluded a little guiltily, *but she doesn't know me, and I don't speak German. I wouldn't have been missed.*

Before long the group arrived at the next destination. With a grimace, Carl trudged through the ankle-deep snow on the unshoveled walk that led to the dark house. Hope rose inside him when no response came to the loud banging on the front door. Maybe he would be home sooner than he thought—and could catch the fourth quarter! But the enthusiasm of the group he was with was undeterred. A small boy, plate of goodies in hand, knocked forcefully again.

Come on. Let's go, already! Carl thought anxiously, shifting his weight from leg to leg. *There aren't any lights on—nobody's home.*

Just as the children had given up and started back down the walk, Carl thought he heard something. His heart dropped. It sounded like the fumbling of a chain lock. He held his breath as everyone stopped and waited. Then, to his utter dismay, the door opened a crack.

"Who's there?" a feeble voice called out from the darkened doorway.

"Why, Sister Klein," came Grandpa's booming response, "it's the Wilson family!"

The boy bearing the cookies shoved them toward the door as if they were some kind of peace offering. The door opened wide, and the frail woman welcomed them into her home.

Sister Klein turned on a small lamp in the living room. It barely illuminated the surrounding area, leaving the rest of the house in shadows. As Carl's eyes slowly adjusted to the dimness, he looked around. The furniture was nice and the room appeared to be clean, but somehow it felt empty. Carl realized that there was no evidence of the upcoming holiday—no tree, no decorations, no presents. But it was even more than that. Something else was missing also. It certainly wasn't the TV. Carl noticed it in the corner of the room, and, for a moment, thoughts of the game filled his head.

I wonder who's winning, he thought irritably, aching to slip over and turn on the TV—just to catch the score. He smiled as he thought of the shocked reaction *that* would get from the others. His smile soon faded as the Wilson clan began singing "Angels We Have Heard on High" with gusto.

When the song was over, all turned toward Sister Klein expectantly. She moved slowly toward Grandma Wilson and embraced her.

"I knew you wouldn't forget me," she said softly, her voice wavering.

"Of course not," Annie's grandma replied kindly, the characteristic smile lighting her face. "Coming to your home is part of our Christmas tradition." Then Grandma sobered. A look of genuine concern replaced her jovial expression. "How are you?"

"Well . . . I honestly haven't felt much like celebrating this holiday season." Sister Klein's eyes began to glisten. "I know it's been eight months since my Charles passed away, but I miss him now more than ever. We spent fifty-two wonderful Christmases together . . . this is our first one apart. It just isn't the same." She brushed away a few stray tears and forced a smile.

Carl looked over at the dark TV once again, but this time he saw the lounge chair situated a few feet in front of it. Maybe tonight Sister Klein's husband would have been watching the game from that very spot. But it was empty—and had been for eight months. That was what was missing. Sister Klein's husband had passed away, leaving her and the home lonely and with a void that was almost tangible.

"Oh, how Charles loved to hear you all sing—he looked forward to it each year. It meant so much to him . . . and to me . . . " Sister Klein began again, but her voice wavered as she hugged those nearest her. "It's good to hear laughter and music in the house again. Please, sing another one, if you have time."

The Wilsons were all too happy to oblige the elderly woman's request, and readied themselves for their encore. Aunt Mary, a clearly gifted pianist, managed to nudge her way through the crowd to the piano at the front of the room. Uncle Adam cleared his throat deeply, then hummed the starting notes so all could find their proper pitch. Before long the group was immersed in the chorus of "O Little Town of Bethlehem."

Carl's face reddened as he tried unsuccessfully to remember the words of the song. *This has got to be some form of torture!* he groaned inwardly, muddling through the remaining verses.

"It's finally starting to feel like Christmas," Sister Klein said quietly when the singing had ended. "Thank you so much for coming." She placed herself at the doorway to bid farewell to her visitors. The group shuffled single file out of the room, receiving a proper embrace from Sister Klein before moving out into the bitter cold. All of the children managed to wiggle past Carl, leaving him to bring up the rear of the long line—and say a final farewell to Sister Klein.

Carl looked around wildly for Annie, hoping she would rescue him, but somehow they had gotten separated and she was nowhere in sight. He watched nervously as the few remaining children hugged Sister Klein, then disappeared through the front door. When there was nobody left to hide behind, Carl took a deep breath and approached her. Feeling as awkward as a bumbling giant, he hovered over her, noticing for the first time how tiny and feeble she really was. But, seemingly undaunted by their size difference, Sister Klein took his hand, her grip weak and trembling. Carl looked down at their clasped hands, amazed at the stark contrast between them. While his was large and robust, hers was gnarled and bony. It was laced with bulging, blue veins and covered only by a layer of paper-thin skin. He stood there, frozen in place, not daring to move his fingers for fear he would break hers.

"Thank you for taking the time to come," Sister Klein said softly, her kind eyes meeting his. "It means a great deal to me."

"Uh—thank you for allowing us into your home," Carl stammered politely, wondering what else he could say. He couldn't lie and say he'd enjoyed himself.

"The pleasure was mine," she replied, her smile emphasizing the deep wrinkles lining her elderly face. At that moment Carl looked past Sister Klein, noticing the picture on the wall behind her for the first time. The Kleins, both full of youth and vibrance, smiled back at him from the black-and-white photo taken at their wedding. With arms wrapped around one another, their faces glowed with happiness and anticipation for the future.

"What a wonderful day that was," Sister Klein sighed, turning to look at the aged picture as well. "It doesn't seem possible that it happened so long ago." She touched it gently, her eyes taking on a faraway look.

"I'm very sorry for your loss," Carl managed to say, surprised at the lump that had suddenly risen in his throat.

"Thank you," she whispered, giving his hand a feeble squeeze before releasing it. "Please, do come again." Carl only nodded, then headed out into the snow.

As the group walked to their next destination, Carl's thoughts remained with Sister Klein and the wedding picture. She had looked so beautiful and full of life, and her husband strong and able-bodied. They were ready to take on the world and make their own future—together. Now, she was old and had only memories. Time had passed and her partner of fifty-two years was gone. It was no wonder she was lonely and needing company.

Carl's mind drifted back to his own wedding. Only six short months had passed since he and his bride had posed for pictures with expressions similar to those of the young Kleins. Carl and Annie had been full of excitement at what lay ahead in their new life together as well. He remembered vividly how her eyes had sparkled that beautiful June morning. The splendor of the bright summer flowers in full bloom had paled in comparison to Annie's radiance. An overwhelming sense of sadness descended upon him. Carl hadn't seen her shine like that in a long time. What had happened to them since their wonderful day? He risked a glance at her, then looked away quickly when their eyes met.

"You're awfully quiet," Annie commented, her voice tentative. "Are you alright?"

"Oh, sure," Carl replied, pulling himself out of his thoughts. "It's just too bad—Sister Klein being alone and all."

"I know. Fifty-two Christmases is a long time to be with someone." Annie fell silent. They walked behind the others with only the sound of crunching snow underfoot and an occasional shout from the children to distract them from their thoughts. Carl couldn't help but wonder if Annie dreaded spending so many years with him. Would they ever make it to their fifty-second Christmas? Together? "So, are you glad we went?" Annie ventured, studying his face as they walked.

"Oh, I don't know about 'glad,'" Carl began, unwilling to admit his deeper feelings. "I mean, going to see her was a nice gesture and all, but did a brief visit and singing a couple of carols really accomplish anything? Wouldn't shoveling her walk do more good? Or changing the oil in her car?" In fact, he could think of several acts of service that would last longer than the fifteen minutes they had spent with her—and that could be done when the game wasn't on.

"But didn't you see the look on her face?" Annie asked in exasperation.

"Yeah, she was happy," Carl retorted, feeling his defenses rise. "But for how long?"

"Longer than a shoveled walk would last in the middle of winter!" Annie said vehemently, then took a deep breath to calm herself. "Sister Klein said it was finally starting to feel like Christmas. What service could be better than that?"

"Look, I'm just offering suggestions," Carl said tightly through his clenched jaw. *Why does she always do this?* He shook his head in frustration, wondering why everything had to turn into an argument with them. *And why am I always the bad guy?* Just then a snowball whizzed past, missing them by less than an inch—and saving Carl from having to further defend himself, at least where Annie was concerned. He whirled instinctively in front of her in an attempt to protect her from the hail of snow pelting them from several directions. Grateful for the diversion, he faced his young assailants while Annie moved safely out of firing range. It wasn't long before the instigators of the snowy brawl, Annie's two youngest brothers, received their just dues.

The snowball fight continued through the streets until a few disgruntled mothers put an end to it. They tried frantically to brush the snow off their boisterous children as the rest of the group waited in front of the Langfords, who were next on the caroling list.

Sister Langford answered, wreathed in smiles as she welcomed them inside. When he saw her, Carl instantly thought of his own mother—an energetic go-getter type that made the most out of life. Sister Langford appeared to be several inches shorter than his mother and was a brunette instead of a blond, yet the two shared the same lean build and Sister Langford looked to be in her early fifties as well.

"Oh, it is so good to see you all!" she exclaimed, her enthusiasm almost disguising the lines of fatigue etched in her face. "A nice visit will do Harold some good. It's been a bit lonely around here since the girls left."

"Are they all settled in then?" Grandma Wilson asked with her usual concern.

"Yes, Betsy is in New Mexico with her little family," Sister Langford began as the group entered her home, "and Mary took a job in Oregon after she graduated in May." The woman continued talking about her children as she ushered the group into the nearby den. For a moment Carl wondered why they were moving out of the formal reception area. Then he entered the next room.

The den, no longer a place for reading and relaxing, had been turned into a hospital room of sorts. Built-in shelves, once a place for books and magazines, were now neatly lined with various medications and folded linens. Brother Langford occupied the center of the room, lying quietly in an adjustable bed with his legs slightly elevated. His eyes were open, but he didn't move or speak to acknowledge his visitors in any way.

"What is *that*?" a little girl with long brown braids asked suddenly, her face aghast. She pointed conspicuously at the partially full catheter bag hanging from the side of the bed. Horrified, her mother shushed the girl while trying to pull her to the back of the room. Everyone stood in embarrassed silence.

"Oh, don't worry about that," Sister Langford said amiably, completely unruffled by the innocent question. "It's perfectly natural to be curious. Our two grandchildren ask about it every time they visit." She wheeled several metal trays covered with tweezers, gauze, and a variety of other supplies out of the way. "Harold, dear," Sister Langford said, turning to her husband, "look who has come to see you!" She patted his arm gently, but Brother Langford still did not react. He stared at the ceiling blankly, just as he had since the group arrived—the rhythmic rise and fall of his chest the only indication that he was still among the living. Sister Langford motioned for everyone to gather around the bedside. "I'm sorry to say he's worsened since you last came. He rarely responds to anything at all now." She looked down quickly to hide her sudden tears, then busied herself with smoothing the wrinkled blankets around him. "But, he always did enjoy hearing you sing when he was coherent," she added after a moment.

With a great feeling of soberness, the Wilson family began with the tender words of "Away in a Manger." Sister Langford sat down next to her husband and held his still hand. He continued to gaze upward, his glassy eyes void of expression.

What happened to this man? Carl wondered, thoughts flooding his mind. It was most likely a stroke that had robbed Brother Langford of his faculties. *But he can't be much more than fifty—about Dad's age.* Carl couldn't help but shake his head as he thought of his father, so active and full of vitality. He often joked that he was finally in the prime of his life and able to enjoy it. And he could still beat Carl in a game of one-on-one basketball without so much as breaking a sweat.

Carl studied the ailing man before him. He was easily over six feet tall, but that was the only physical trait comparable to Carl's father. Brother Langford was barely more than a skeleton, his long frame thin and frail. The flesh hung from his bare arms, no longer filled out with any kind of muscle mass. Sharp cheek bones jutted out of his gaunt face, and his lifeless eyes were dark and hollow.

He shouldn't be in that bed! Carl's heart ached as he thought of all that Brother Langford was missing. *He should be able to play in the snow with his grandkids and go for walks with his wife.* Carl watched Sister Langford as she affectionately squeezed her husband's hand. *What a strong woman she must be,* Carl concluded in admiration.

At that moment a thought hit him with such force that Carl almost staggered. His stomach clenched into a tight knot as he looked at Annie beside him. What if she had to be burdened by him in such a way? And at such an early age? It was expected that one spouse would ultimately care for the other in their declining years, but at age fifty or fifty-five? What would give Annie the strength that Sister Langford possessed to endure? With heavy heart he realized he hadn't given his wife many reasons to want to love and nurture him now when he was young and healthy, let alone later in life. He hoped with all of his heart that Annie would never have to go through such a trial. Yet, he realized he would gladly care for her, if the need arose.

Suddenly the image of the Kleins' wedding photo came vividly to his mind. Looking around him, Carl felt an overwhelming urge to see a picture of the Langfords. He wanted to know what the couple looked like in happier times, when life was full of hope—some kind of evidence that Sister Langford had cherished memories to sustain her through this trying time. Carl searched the room from where he stood, but it was in vain. There were no pictures on the walls or surrounding shelves.

Just as he was about to give up, several small frames arranged on one of the rolling trays caught his attention. Straining his eyes to make out the details, he studied the pictures across the room. The first was a family photo, featuring the Langfords in the center with a grandchild on each lap and their children standing behind them. The second was a simple snapshot of Brother Langford thigh-deep in the midst of a large stream, sporting waders and proudly holding up a prized rainbow trout for all to see. The last was a portrait of Brother and Sister Langford looking at each other tenderly, happiness glowing in their faces. Although no wedding photograph was on display, Carl had found what he was looking for. The pictures provided proof that building a life and family together had created a source of strength from which the Langfords could draw in their time of adversity.

Deep in his own thoughts, Carl had long since tuned out the singing around him—until the beginning of the third verse. Then the lyrics registered in his mind with sudden clarity as he looked back at Brother Langford.

"*Be near me, Lord Jesus; I ask thee to stay . . .*" The words rang out poignantly as Carl searched Brother Langford's face. Carl held his breath. He thought he had seen movement, but was he mistaken?

"*. . . Close by me forever, and love me, I pray . . .*" No—there it was again. Brother Langford had blinked. At first just once, then twice more. Then he began blinking slowly but steadily. Annie, also aware of what was happening, grabbed Carl's hand and squeezed it tightly. They watched in amazement as Sister Langford, with tears spilling down her cheeks, stroked her husband's face fervently.

Does he understand the meaning of the song? Carl's mind reeled as he contemplated the possibility. *Maybe Brother Langford understands more than we know. Maybe he just can't make himself understood.* He hadn't responded until the third verse. The significance of those words had not eluded Carl. *Be near me, Lord Jesus; I ask thee to stay close by me forever, and love me, I pray . . .* the words echoed in his head. Maybe the message of the song was the desire of Brother Langford's heart. Carl could think of no greater comfort than to have the Savior close by during a time of such affliction.

By now most everyone had noticed Brother Langford's response, and the singing had stopped completely. A few muffled sobs and sniffles could be heard as the group struggled with the emotional scene before them. Then, several voices began again in an attempt to finish the song, but the last few words came out choked and strangled. Swallowing hard, Carl barely managed to keep his own tears at bay.

When the singing was over, Brother Langford stared blankly at the ceiling once again. It was as if nothing had happened—but the Wilsons had seen it. Carl had seen it. At that moment a new thought came to him. It wasn't only the words of the song that had touched Brother Langford. Carl was sure that merely quoting the verse wouldn't have brought about any reaction at all—but the words carried through music had stirred Brother Langford's soul. It was *singing* that had broken through the haze that clouded the man's mind, if only for a moment.

Carl now knew that shoveling snow or changing oil, though both good and needed services, would not have caused such a response. Brother Langford would have been completely unaware that such acts had ever been done. Although the level of his understanding would never be known, he had shown that he was aware of human voices joined in song around him. It was a heartfelt service done with only one purpose—to show him love. He'd responded to nothing else while the Wilsons were in his home.

With full hearts, the group left the Langford home and moved toward the next destination. The mood was noticeably different now. There was an air of quiet reverence about the Wilson family that wasn't present before.

Carl was grateful for the stillness as he silently wrestled with the feelings churning inside him. Guilt and shame tore away at him as thoughts of Sister Langford caring for her invalid husband night and day plagued his mind. She truly knew what it meant to serve to the point of exhaustion. Carl was only giving up one evening of his time to bring cheer to those in need, yet he had been bitter about it from the start.

Carl looked up from the gray slush on the street and caught sight of Annie. He studied her as she walked ahead with her sister, talking softly and nodding every now and then. Completely unaware of his gaze, she smiled broadly about something in the conversation. Carl held his breath. Although he could only see her profile, he knew that smile, and his heart skipped a beat. Drawing upon a memory of that same expression, he closed his eyes and reveled in it. When Annie smiled, she didn't just turn up the corners of her mouth. Her whole face became part of it, from the slight dimples in her cheeks to the tiny lines that appeared around her twinkling eyes. At that moment Carl would have given anything to know what had brought that expression to her face. It was something he rarely saw anymore, and that could only mean one thing—Annie wasn't happy. Maybe she was right. Maybe they *were* too different.

Unwilling to accept that possibility, Carl began to search himself for the answers to what had gone wrong in his marriage and his life. With sinking heart he thought of the countless times he'd been unwilling to bend or accommodate even Annie's most simple requests. Just yesterday she had told him about her upcoming company Christmas party. Without even thinking, he had refused to go because he wouldn't know anyone and it was sure to be long and boring. Tonight he hadn't wanted to come because he didn't want to miss the game or do anything that might make him look like a fool. Carl felt sick to his stomach as other examples jumped into his head that only emphasized his appalling discovery—his own comfort and wants came before the happiness of his wife. The realization brought him to one conclusion: he was selfish.

His friend Brian had said a little more Christmas spirit would do Carl some good. But Carl was sure it was going to take more than that to help him.

"It's a beautiful night," Grandpa Wilson commented, falling in step with Carl. "Cold, but clear."

"Uh . . . yeah—beautiful," Carl stammered, completely startled. So wrapped up in his own thoughts, he hadn't noticed Grandpa slow his stride. "What happened to Brother Langford?"

"He suffered an aneurysm a little over a year ago," Grandpa said softly. "He was working out in the yard—his wife found him lying on the ground. It took everyone by surprise."

Carl nodded sadly. "I can imagine." They walked in silence as Carl processed the information. He really couldn't imagine how awful that would be. "Does Sister Langford care for her husband alone?" he finally asked.

"Mostly," Grandpa replied. "But he's too heavy for her to lift. She can't move him on her own. Some of the men in the neighborhood help when she gives Brother Langford a bath or the sheets need to be changed. Things like that."

Carl just nodded, knowing that Grandpa Wilson was too humble to admit that he was one of those men.

After a long pause, Carl asked, "How long have you been caroling?"

"Well, now," Grandpa responded thoughtfully, "as long as we've lived here. I guess we're coming up on forty years!" He laughed heartily at Carl's shocked expression. "Quite a tradition, wouldn't you say?"

"It most certainly is," Carl agreed, his admiration and respect growing even more for the stalwart man beside him.

"But I must confess," Grandpa said, chuckling quietly, "caroling wasn't my idea at all. Grandma *insisted* we do it every year. And, it took quite a lot of coaxing to get me out here the first few years—to say the least!" Grandpa laughed at Carl's surprise. "I would have much rather stayed at home than traipse through these streets in miserable December weather." He clapped Carl on the shoulder, then gave him a knowing look. "But, I've managed to get into the spirit of it since then."

"I didn't know," Carl said thoughtfully, wondering why Grandpa had confessed this to him. Was it because Carl's reluctance was so transparent? Why hadn't he tried harder to hide his discomfort? He glanced down in embarrassment.

"You also never know what will change a person." Grandpa's eyes twinkled as Carl looked back at him blankly.

"What do you mean?" Carl asked, wondering what exactly Grandpa was referring to. How could caroling really *change* anyone? He could now see the value of such a service—the joy in the faces of those they had visited was proof of that. Carl no longer disputed that caroling could make someone happy. But was that what Grandpa meant? Or was he implying that hearing a few songs could make a significant difference in someone's life?

"You'll figure it out," Grandpa said, then called for the attention of the rest of the group. "This is the last stop!" he announced as the family gathered outside of the Brenchley home. For one final time, a plate of goodies, looking more sloppy than ever, was sent to the door.

"Come in, come in!" Brother Brenchley called out jovially when the nearly frozen bunch had congregated on his doorstep. "I've been expecting you!" he stepped aside to allow passage into the warmth of his home. Once everyone had entered, Brother Brenchley closed the door, then carefully made his way into the living room with one hand placed against the wall to guide him. Carl watched, curious as to why the man did so.

"By the sound of all those footsteps, I can tell your family has grown in numbers! There must be at least thirty of you here!" Brother Brenchley said.

"There are *thirty-four* of us to be exact!" Grandpa Wilson said proudly, then began detailing what each family had been up to over the last few months.

Carl studied Brother Brenchley as he stood at the front of the room. He didn't focus on anyone or anything. Instead he gazed upward slightly with his head tilted toward Grandpa Wilson. It was obvious to Carl that Brother Brenchley was listening intently.

"Ah, what a posterity you have—and ever growing!" he began when Grandpa had finished. Then he moved carefully toward the group. "My eyesight is gone—along with my youth, but I don't need to see you kids to know how much you've grown!"

He's blind, Carl thought in amazement. He never would have guessed from merely looking at Brother Brenchley.

The man's eyes were not cloudy or glazed, but alive and animated. He didn't use a cane or any device other than his hand to guide him about the home. But, as surprising as it seemed, he was definitely blind.

Bewildered, Carl watched as Brother Brenchley placed his hand gently on top of each small head. Grandpa Wilson then stated the child's name and whom he belonged to. Brother Brenchley paused, then nodded every time as if he were taking meticulous notes in his head. "They're all sprouting up like weeds," he laughed heartily when he had come to the end of the line. "I can't believe this is the same group that came last year!"

Carl then realized what Brother Brenchley was doing. Because he no longer had the use of his eyes, he was using his hands to "see" the children and to measure their growth. Carl had never witnessed anything like it.

The children then shuffled to the back, allowing the adults to move forward. Brother Brenchley shook each hand firmly and spent a few moments catching up on the year's events.

When he reached Carl, he clasped his hand, then paused. "I don't believe we've met," he said amiably.

"I married Annie, the Wilsons' granddaughter," Carl explained, amazed at Brother Brenchley's perception. "My name is Carl."

"Well, congratulations! You've joined a wonderful family," Brother Brenchley stated, then turned to face the rest of the group. "Now, I believe you came to sing?"

"Yes indeed. Do you have a request?" Grandpa Wilson asked.

"I've long loved the carol 'Silver Bells,'" Brother Brenchley said without hesitation. "And if memory serves, your family sings it beautifully."

The Wilsons quickly shuffled into place and, after humming a few notes, began the familiar song. Brother Brenchley joined in, his deep voice blending perfectly. They all sang in unison until the chorus, and then their voices split into full, rich harmony.

As Carl looked around, he really noticed the children for the first time that evening. Just moments before they had been scampering noisily all over the neighborhood. Now they stood in a crowded line, trying to keep from fidgeting, and singing with all of the enthusiasm they could muster. Carl realized these little ones had sung with all of their hearts and participated eagerly at each home they had visited. He hadn't heard any of them complain, though by now they had to be tired and hungry, especially at their ages.

Except ye be converted, and become as little children, ye shall not enter into the kingdom of heaven . . . The words from the book of Matthew came painfully to his mind. Carl remembered his own childhood, when he was teachable and open to new experiences. What had happened to him since then? When had he become so unwilling to change, or even compromise?

At the end of the first verse Brother Brenchley paused for a moment, then took a deep breath. Pulling a handkerchief from his pocket, he wiped his eyes and coughed into it several times. Then all was silent while the Wilsons waited for him to finish the song.

"I'm sorry," Brother Brenchley began, then stopped, unable to say anything more. He motioned for the others to continue.

The song concluded, but Brother Brenchley still did not speak. He stood there quietly while tears flowed freely from his unseeing eyes.

"Thank you," he whispered after regaining his composure somewhat. "Thank you for taking time for me. Thank you for caring about me."

Carl felt as if Brother Brenchley's gaze was focused upon him. Although he knew that was impossible, it was as if the man were looking right at Carl and talking directly to him. A lump rose in Carl's throat for the second time that evening.

As the group reluctantly filed out of the home, Carl once again found himself at the end of the line. He felt ashamed as he and Brother Brenchley clasped hands once again. Although Carl's physical features and stature would remain unseen, he felt sure that Brother Brenchley could discern far more about him—maybe even enough to know what was in his heart. And Carl wasn't ready for that—not yet.

"Thank *you* for coming, Carl." Brother Brenchley squeezed Carl's hand tightly before loosening his grip, then leaned in closer. "It means a lot to an old man."

"I'm glad I came," Carl answered truthfully, though the experience had left him in turmoil. And he couldn't help but wonder which of the two of them was really blind.

Carl joined the others as they walked toward the Wilson house in silence. They weren't in a hurry despite the plummeting temperatures, and there were no snowballs flying or children wrestling. A sweet feeling of peace had enveloped the family, and no one wanted to dispel it. Although Carl could feel the serenity of those around him, he didn't share in it.

What do I do? Carl wondered, growing more distressed with each passing moment. *Can I change? Or is it too late?* He had to face the fact that maybe too much damage had been done—maybe Annie had already decided to give up on him entirely. The thought was sickening and it made his head reel. *No, she wouldn't do it,* he tried to convince himself. *She wouldn't leave me.* Yet, in the back of his mind, the possibility was very real—and he couldn't blame her if she did choose to go.

At that moment Carl remembered something he had learned multiple times throughout his years of schooling. Every living thing had two basic responses to conflict, and he had to choose between them now. Fight or flight—it was that simple. For a moment, the last option seemed the most attractive. It would be the easiest way out, and his pride would remain intact. He could just run away from change. Not having to admit he was wrong and rationalizing his actions away would mean that life would go on as usual. After all, he wasn't that bad a guy. He worked hard and provided for their needs, and he certainly wasn't mean or abusive.

But . . . The word stuck out in his mind like a giant billboard on the freeway. The "flight" option would also mean living in the same house, but with separate lives—more like roommates than husband and wife. They would come and go, barely speaking to each other as the rift between them grew larger. Sooner or later one of them would decide to move on to a greener pasture—or they would just be miserable for the rest of their lives. That option suddenly lost its appeal.

So, Carl was left with the only other choice. He could fight. He had to fight. But now he had to fight *for* their marriage instead of *against* it. He had to do everything in his power to change, no matter how hard or long the process might be. He had to beg Annie for forgiveness and plead for another chance—a chance to make things right between them and to find the happiness they both desperately wanted.

But what if she wouldn't listen? What if she turned him away? The possibility caused him to shudder.

All too soon, Carl found himself in front of the Wilson home. He stepped back into the shadows, not wanting to mingle with the family quite yet. Hoping that he would go unnoticed, he held his breath as everyone headed up the walk and to the front door. The prospects of warmth and refreshments lured the group, including Annie, quickly inside. Much to Carl's relief, he was left alone. After a few minutes, he ventured over to the steps and sat down. Blowing warm air into his hands, he shivered as the chill of the cement penetrated his jeans and moved throughout his body.

But the cold was soon forgotten as Carl sat on the porch, staring up at the dark expanse of sky above him. His thoughts turned to the people they had visited. He remembered Sister Schmidt. What kind of courage had it taken for her to leave her home? How hard was it for her to face each day, unable to understand anyone but her daughter? Even something as simple as going to the store was probably a difficult challenge for her.

Sister Klein was faced with a great trial as well. She had to find the willpower to go on living each day without the companionship of her lifelong sweetheart. *The hours must pass so slowly for her,* Carl contemplated sadly. *The days must drag on forever as she waits to be reunited with her husband.*

Then Carl remembered the Langfords. Sister Langford had strength and faith beyond Carl's comprehension. For her, every waking moment was filled with doing acts of service. Brother Langford spent his days held prisoner by his incapacitated body.

Finally Brother Brenchley came to mind. He braved the challenge of living in a world void of color and light, but could still find beauty though darkness surrounded him. The faces of his visitors had remained unseen that evening, but he didn't need to see them to feel of their love. And though his sight had been clouded by time, it was Brother Brenchley who could *really* see and understand—even more so than Carl. Brother Brenchley had the Spirit with him. Carl could feel it. And with the Spirit, Brother Brenchley didn't need to rely on human eyes to see.

Hope began to glimmer inside of Carl's heart. If these people could face their challenges every day with the strength to endure, so could Carl. He could find the courage to face Annie and admit that he had been terribly wrong. He could ask her for help as he made the necessary changes to bring happiness to them both. But first, he needed help from another source.

Oh, Father, Carl pleaded in silent prayer. *Please forgive me!* He felt the warmth of a tear as it escaped and slid slowly down his cheek. His blessings began flooding his mind. He could communicate, he was strong and healthy, he had his sight, and he hadn't lost Annie yet. With so many blessings in his life, how could he have allowed himself to fall into the snare of selfishness and pride? *Please help me to change,* he prayed over and over again.

Until that moment Carl had been staring blankly across the yard, looking at nothing in particular. Then, slowly the details of the house across the street began to register in his mind. It wasn't that the home was extraordinary in any way; it looked much like the others they had visited or passed that evening. But for some reason, Carl saw everything about it differently—the decorated tree in the window, the blinking lights outlining the rooftop, and the evergreen wreath placed on the front door. They were all signs of the most celebrated holiday of the year—signs that Carl usually ignored.

Tonight it was different for him. The tree seemed to stand taller and the lights appeared to burn brighter than any he had ever seen. It was as if they were calling Carl's attention to something he hadn't given much thought to for many years—the reason for all of the decorations and celebration, the reason for Christmas.

Christmas was about Jesus Christ. He'd truly been born in a humble stable and had lived His life among men. He'd brought the world out of darkness and given men hope that all could be freed from sin and death. Carl reflected on the fact that Christmas was a reminder for everyone to be more like Christ. It was about giving of oneself—not just during the holidays, but every day.

Carl had been taught the meaning of Christmas since he was a child, but he had forgotten how it affected him personally. Lately, the Christmas story had been just that—a story. It was something he heard every Christmas Eve, and though he knew it was a true story, it wasn't fully part of him. But now his mind filled with new understanding and his heart swelled with gratitude. Christ had come to save *all* mankind—including Carl. Because of Jesus, Carl could be forgiven.

This Christmas held another meaning for Carl. It meant an opportunity to start over, a chance to heal the past. The timing was perfect, he realized with some excitement. It was his first Christmas with Annie and he vowed to make it a happy one. Now he was sure a little more Christmas spirit would do him some good.

"You know you're going to freeze out here." Annie's voice broke the stillness. Carl stood and wheeled around, nearly falling off the bottom step.

"Oh—hi," he stammered. "I didn't hear you come out."

"Obviously," she said, a slight smile playing on her lips. "I brought you some hot chocolate."

"Thank you." He shivered involuntarily as the heat from the cup warmed his hands.

"Did you want to come in?" Annie asked. "Everyone's asking where you are—and the game is just ending. I'm sure you don't want to miss that." The edge in her voice was subtle, but unmistakable. For a moment Carl felt the familiar rise of tension, and the urge to come back with a sarcastic remark was hard to suppress, but he took a deep breath.

"I would rather stay out here with you," he replied calmly, although he was pleading for divine help in his mind. Annie's mouth parted but no sound came out. Carl had to hold back a chuckle as she stared at him doubtfully. He moved from the stairs and faced her. "There are a few things I need to tell you."

"Okay," Annie said cautiously, looking as though she no longer recognized him. "I'm listening."

"Well, um . . ." Now it was Carl's turn to look baffled. Where was he supposed to start? "I'm sorry—so, so sorry," he began, wishing he had a more eloquent speech prepared. "For being inconsiderate, insensitive, and . . . selfish." Feeling utterly ridiculous for his inability to express himself, he waited for her to say something. When she didn't respond, he rushed on. "I've been so wrapped up in myself, I didn't realize how I've changed—and how much I was hurting you." He paused, but Annie remained silent. *Please say something! Anything!* Panic seized him as he stared at the blank expression on her face. Usually her eyes gave her feelings away, but at that moment they seemed void of emotion and he couldn't read them.

As scared as he was, Carl knew he couldn't give up, no matter what Annie's reaction might be—at least not until he had said everything he needed to say. "Please forgive me," he plunged in again. "I know it's a lot to ask, but please, if you possibly can, forgive me." Completely aware that he was shamelessly begging, he rushed on. "And if I'm blessed enough to be by your side for the next fifty-two Christmases, I'll spend every one of them making it up to you. I'll even go caroling—I want to go caroling."

Tears stung his eyes as he waited for a reply, but Annie just stood there, frozen in place without so much as batting an eye.

"I don't know what else to say." Carl looked down in defeat, unable to meet her gaze any longer. With an overwhelming sense of dread, he said the only thing left to say. "I love you, Annie . . . and I don't know how I can live without you, but I can't—I mean I *won't* go on making you miserable." He put the mug down and turned to walk away.

"Do you want to check the score?" Annie asked quietly. Carl stopped midway down the stairs, his back still toward her.

"What?!" he asked in disbelief. Didn't she hear anything he'd said? Didn't she understand? Not that he could blame her. He would have had a hard time believing himself if he were her.

"The score . . . of the game," Annie said, her voice barely audible.

"It doesn't matter." He choked back a sob. "The game doesn't matter." As far as he was concerned, nothing mattered anymore.

As Carl took another step down, he felt her hand on his shoulder. Squeezing his eyes shut against the pain, he stopped, then slowly turned to face her.

"It does matter—if it's important to you," Annie whispered, her lip trembling. "I just didn't understand that until now." In an instant Annie was in his arms, her head buried against Carl's chest. He stood there holding her, feeling dazed and unsure of what she meant to say. But as she clung to him more tightly, the significance of her words dawned on him and his heart soared. Annie was telling him that she wanted to compromise. She was trying to find some middle ground.

"I'll catch the highlights later," Carl murmured, wanting to laugh and cry at the same time. For a long time neither one of them spoke, both content to savor the moment and the closeness of each other.

"Annie," Carl said finally, pulling away just enough to look at her. Gently, he wiped her tears away. "I know change takes time—all of our problems won't be solved overnight. But—"

"You're not the only one who needs to change," Annie interrupted, placing her hand over his mouth. "I've been impatient, defensive, hard to live with . . . I know the list goes on." As Carl opened his mouth to object, she shushed him again. "We're both to blame. But if we're willing to work together . . . and help each other, I know we'll make it. And I know we can be happy."

Carl looked deeply into Annie's eyes once again, this time finding all of the emotion that had been vacant just moments before. Her face glowed with the same commitment he felt.

"Should we go inside?" he asked, though he was reluctant to share her with anyone else right then.

"No, let's go home," Annie said as she put her arm around his waist and started down the steps. "I already said good-bye for the both of us." She looked up at him and smiled her glorious smile. "Besides, we have a lot of catching up to do."

"You never know what will change a person . . ." Grandpa Wilson's words echoed in Carl's head as he and Annie walked to the car. Carl couldn't help but smile. Grandpa wasn't referring to Sister Schmidt, Sister Klein, or any of the others they had visited. He was talking about himself—and about Carl. Grandpa was talking about the change of heart that came about through serving others.

After opening the car door for Annie, Carl chuckled to himself as he walked around to his side. Shaking his head in disbelief, he thought of how drastically his feelings had changed in just one night. Carl had gone caroling with the idea that he was doing everyone else a favor, but in reality, he had received the greatest blessing that evening. Laughing out loud, he felt a sudden urge to sing "We Wish You a Merry Christmas."

Carl opened the car door and was just about to get in when he noticed a few fluffy snowflakes floating softly in the dark, December night. He watched as each one landed gently on the clean, shoveled sidewalk.

ABOUT THE AUTHOR

Author Julie Warnick served a mission to Barcelona, Spain, and shortly after her return she met her husband Quin. Eight and a half years later they are the proud parents of two beautiful daughters with a third child on the way. Julie's interest in writing began just after her first daughter, Emily, was four months old. The author started writing the Christmas story *Light of Bethlehem* to pass the time while Emily napped. Now that Emily is five, her sister Hannah nearly three, and a new baby joining the family soon, free time is a thing of the past for Mommy. But Julie has discovered the joy of writing and occasionally manages to find a few minutes in between laundry and dishes to write. She loves spending time with her family, scrapbooking, quilting, reading, and traveling. She and her family live in Orem.

Author's note

My grandparents started Christmas caroling to neighbors when their own children were young. The tradition that started out as a family of nine singing from house to house, grew to include grandchildren and great-grandchildren.

Our family went every Christmas until recently; my grandmother's health began to fail a few years ago, and she passed away in November of 2003. Although she is greatly missed, I am thankful she is at peace and no longer suffering. The memory of my grandmother will remain alive in the hearts of many because of the acts of service she performed while she was able.

The ideas for *A Caroling Christmas* came from our family tradition, but this story is a work of fiction. The characters and situations are not intended to be construed as actual people and events.